Litle Brother of the Wilderness

THE STORY of JOHNNY APPLESEED

JB
CHA

Published in the United States by Holy Cow! Press, 5435
Old Highway 18, Stevens Point, Wisconsin 54481.

We gratefully acknowledge the assistance and
encouragement of Joseph W. Grant for this project.

Library of Congress Cataloging-in-Publication Data

Le Sueur, Meridel
  Little brother of the wilderness.

   Summary: Recounts the story of the man who carried apple seeds and
started apple orchards throughout the midwestern states.
   1. Appleseed, Johnny, 1774-1845—Juvenile literature. 2. Apple
growers—United States—Biography—Juvenile literature. 3. Frontier
and pioneer life—Middle West—Juvenile literature. (1. Appleseed,
Johnny, 1774-1845. 2. Apple growers. 3. Frontier and pioneer life)
I. Sansom, Suzy, ill. II. Title.
SB63.C46L2   1987   634'.11'0924 (B) (92)   87-80574
ISBN 0-930100-21-2

This project is supported in part by a grant from the
National Endowment for the Arts in Washington, D.C., a
Federal agency.

For DEBORAH

whose mother was a mare
her sister a fawn,
her brother a duck.
And who always walked
in the tender world of
the wilderness where
flowers spring up.

It was lonely making America. It was a big, big country. It was a deep, wide country.

And there were no apple trees.

There were no apple trees blooming in the spring, no big round apples, no little bright tart apples.

No apples at all!

This was very sad.

It would have been very sad to this day, but there was a man who thought it would be very lonely making America without any apple trees blooming early in the spring, without red apples hanging on the trees in Ohio, Illinois, and Iowa, in the frosty fall.

He thought it would be lonely making America without apple trees, apple butter, apple cider and apple pies, while men were chopping out the forest, ploughing up the prairies, planting wheat and corn in North America.

This man's name was Jonathan Chapman.

My Grandmother in Ohio saw him going by her house in the spring, in the fall. The geese flying in a wedge in the sky looked down and saw him traveling along, wearing his gunny sack coat, his books stuffed in front of it, and on his head his stewpot hat to keep him cool in the heat of the day. When night came he cooked his mush in it. He never wore any shoes if he could help it.

*My grandmother in Ohio saw him going by her house
in the Spring . . .*

The swans, the ducks and the blue herons saw him.

The little quails walking in the prairie grass low down on the earth, saw his big bare feet and they said to each other, "There he goes looking after his apple trees."

For Jonathan Chapman was a lean and lonesome man who loved apples.

He was a man who never threw an apple core away in his life.

When he was a young man he was walking in Pennsylvania. In those early days Pennsylvania was about the last place where people lived. Beyond was the wilderness. The animals and Indians lived in the wilderness and the wild herbs grew and the tall trees stood in the lonesome wind.

Jonathan stopped to get something to eat and he heard a child crying from a covered wagon which was going on into the wilderness.

The child was crying to his mother, "I don't want to go. I want to stay here."

The child's mother was angry. She said, "You can't stay here. Your father is going West. And you must go West too."

The child cried, "I don't want to leave the apple trees. The apples will be hanging from the trees. The apples will be getting ripe. I want to stay with the apples."

Jonathan said to the crying child, "I love apple trees too. They are my children. I love apples because they have such kind hearts. The trees are so generous. A tree has not one blossom but thousands. If God made no other fruit but the apple His work would have been well done. Don't cry child. I will plant thousands of tiny seeds in the wilderness where you are going, in Illinois, in Indiana, in Kentucky, and the apple trees will spring up and bloom in the spring."

So the child stopped crying and smiled at Jonathan . . .

So the child stopped crying and smiled at Jonathan and waved from the back of the covered wagon as they went into the wilderness, into the land of the Indian and the snake, of the buffalo and the deep grass.

The land that had no apple trees.

Jonathan was standing by a cider mill. He saw big piles of apple mash and in the mash were all the tiny brown apple seeds. He had a bright idea.

Jonathan got a sack and sat down and began to pick each seed out of the apple mash and put it into the sack.

A man came along and said, "What are you doing?"

Jonathan said, "I am going to fill this sack with apple seeds."

The man said, "And what are you going to do with a sack of apple seeds?"

"I am going to follow the covered wagons out of town toward the sun," Jonathan said. "I am going to plant them. The soil must be good there and the children are crying for apples."

And the man laughed. "What an idea, carrying seed like a bird!"

Others by this time had gathered, and they were all laughing at Jonathan squatting in the mash putting apple seeds into a sack.

"Ho!" they laughed. "Look at him! What's your name?"

"Johnny," he answered them.

"Ho!" the men laughed. "Johnny, Johnny Appleseed!"

So that was what he was called after that, my Grandmother told me—Johnny Appleseed.

*. . . they were all laughing at Jonathan squatting
in the mash . . .*

The children ran out, when he came into the village clearings in the wilderness, shouting, "Here comes Johnny Appleseed."

The deer came with him to the edge of the forest and said, "Goodbye, Johnny Appleseed."

The little round eyes of the robin, the wren, the marsh birds and the swans saw him walking with his pack of apple seeds on his back and they knew Johnny Appleseed was going by.

He followed the sun every day, lying down in the fields at night; rising, walking west with the sun. And on his back he carried a gunny sack, and in the sack thousands of apple seeds went with him, which would be great trees along the valley by the time you were born.

And all the animals knew, all the birds and the buffalo and the deer and the bear knew that he carried a shovel, an ax, and a hoe, but never a gun.

My Grandmother told me too that he never carried a gun. My Grandmother said that he was the friend of all the beasts and birds of the American wilderness.

He never carried a gun at all.

My Grandmother told me it was a very wild country then. There were Indians. There were valleys and woods full of snakes. There were wild animals. But Johnny Appleseed never raised his hand against them and they came to know that he was going to plant his apple seeds on the edge of the wilderness where all the people who got lonely going so far away from home would see them blooming in the spring and feel better.

All the women would lift their hands and cry out, "Apple trees! Just like home!"

And the children would begin to hippity-

hop and yell, "Apples! Apples!"
O, the bright golden apple!
O, the rich juicy apple!

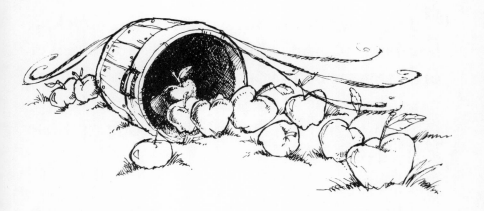

It was early spring in Licking Creek, Ohio, my Grandmother said, when she first saw Johnny Appleseed coming through the forest with his pack of apple seeds in a sack over his shoulder.

He was tall, she said, skinny, with long black hair falling to his bony shoulders. But it was the eyes, she said, you couldn't forget. He carried a hoe and an ax, she said, but he never carried a gun which was a very strange thing in those days.

There was one store in Licking Creek, a few houses, and when you crossed the river on the ferryboat you went into the wilderness, into the dark forest. Licking Creek, Ohio, was as far as people had gone in those early days.

The child ran from his mother crying, "The apple man!"

Johnny said to the child, "I told you I'd come bringing apples."

The store man said, "What have you got in your sack, friend? Must be mighty heavy."

"No," Johnny said, "it's pretty light."

"Is it gold?" the store man said.

"No, it's apple seeds," Johnny said.

"Apple seeds!" the child said laughing.

"Apple seeds!" the store keeper said. "I'll swan, apple seeds! Let's take a look."

The child and the store man in Licking

Creek, Ohio, looked into the sack and saw thousands of tiny seeds with their cheeks against each other, longing to be trees.

"What are you going to do, friend?" the store keeper said.

"He's going to plant the seeds," the child said, "so the apple trees will grow."

"That's right," Johnny said. "I aim to plant them in some rich soft friendly earth so that the lonely settlers will always have apple trees by their cabin doors."

"Well, I'll swan!" the store keeper said. "I'll swan! We do need apples in these parts. We need apples mightily."

My Grandmother said that they all went with Johnny Appleseed right then and there as he walked along the river looking for a good warm place to plant the apple seeds that would grow up into great apple orchards long before you were born.

The hunters didn't go hunting that morning.

The river men came to see what was up.

The trappers left their traps and the frontiersmen waited to see what was happening.

The animals wondered why nobody came to shoot them that morning. And they all looked out of the wilderness to see what was happening.

The birds watched from the treetops.

The deer slid along the shadows, watching.

The tiny things under the leaves—the snails, the worms, the dying butterflies—watched.

The rabbits sat up silently, watching.

And they all wondered why no hunters came; why no shots were fired. Why were all the traps waiting?

At last Johnny stopped. The child

stopped. The animals stopped.

"This is a good place," Johnny said. "This is good earth for growing apples."

With his ax he cleared off a spot where the sun was bright and the soil rich.

With his shovel he dug it up and made the loam soft.

Then he leaned over and the child walked with him, dropping apple seeds in neat rows, so that many little trees would grow up.

The hunter leaned from his saddle. All the animals moved with alarm. He asked, "Expect those seeds to grow? The deer will eat them in no time, and if the deer don't eat them the rabbits will, or the chipmunks or the racoons will surely do what the rabbits don't do."

Johnny said, "I'll make a tight brush fence. The animals won't touch them. We have an understanding."

The animals all moved nearer to watch Johnny and the child make a tight brush fence.

Johnny straightened up and said, "I'll be back in a year and you'll see that by the time the settlers come and this is a TOWN, they can all have apple trees and set them out at their cabin doors."

"Shall I sell them the trees?" asked the store keeper, who was always thinking of selling something.

"Sell them or not," Johnny Applesaid said, "but see that they all have apple trees."

"I'll watch them" the child said walking along with him down to the river towards the ferryboat.

And the hunter, and the trapper all scratched their heads as they watched Johnny Appleseed, standing on the ferry that would take him across the Ohio River into

*. . . and the child walked with him, dropping apple
seeds in neat rows . . .*

the wilderness. They heard his voice singing across the morning.

> I love the golden apples that
>   hang upon the tree.
> Heigho! the apple tree is good
>   enough for me.
> Some folks like the peach tree,
> Some folks like the cherry,
> Some folks like the grape and wine,
> To make them merry.
> But give me rich ripe apples
> Wherever I may be,
> Heigho! the apple tree
> Is good enough for me.

Across the sunlight on the other shore they saw him raise his stewpot hat, waving them farewell.

My Grandmother said that a crow had

flown ahead and told the animals that a man was coming without a gun to shoot them with.

She said the birds, except those who sleep all day like the owls, flew along with him.

And the deer loped silently behind him through the trackless wilderness.

My Grandmother always told me this was
a very big country. At that time most of it was
wilderness. She said it was very lonely, very
often. She said they used to sing to them-
selves out there on the prairie:

> Fifty miles east to a house.
> Fifty miles west to a house.
> Fifty miles north to a friend.
> Fifty miles south to a neighbor.
> Six inches down to bedrock.

But Johnny Appleseed was not lonely. He walked back and forth across the country like a shuttler tending his apple trees. He went into the wilderness, out of the wilderness. He was in the snake and the buffalo country, into the tall grass and the short grass country, through the forests, down the rivers.

With him walked the animals, and above him flew his friends the birds, and deep down in the tall grass and the short grass, the tiny eyes of quails saw him. Worms and snails moved out of the way of his toes. All the crawling, creeping, stinging things watched Johnny Appleseed going by, wearing the morning and the evening light, reading the sky, with a hoe instead of a gun.

They all said, "There goes Johnny Appleseed, going back for seed, or going West to plant them, with one pants' leg blue and the other one red, his cup, the palm of his hand."

Sometimes in the forest the Indians would see him sitting in a clearing with the noses of deer on his knees and he would be telling them that all animals are brothers and should live together in the forest in peace.

When he saw fear in their eyes he knew why they were afraid. The eyes of the deer told him, "Great Noise waits behind the trees for us. While we are standing in the grass by the water one of us—brother, sister, mother—drops to the earth and never rises again, killed by Great Noise."

"We are trapped," said the rabbit, "in the brush, in the grass. There are jaws that snap our running legs."

The wolf told him, "There are big traps that close on us and then the two-legged one comes and takes away our brothers."

"It is sad, my brothers," Johnny told them. "You will have to go farther into the wilderness. America is being built and you will hear the sound of the ax and the sound of many people. The building of America is a mighty song. But it is not for your ears. You will have to go into the wilderness."

Once in the winter he was walking through the snow, looking for a place to stay all night. He had a way of wearing one shoe, breaking the crust of ice and then letting his bare foot follow after.

Having no friend he very often talked to his feet. He would say to the left foot, "You won't get to wear the shoe today because you stumbled over that log in the Maumee River yesterday. You are a very bad foot. Today you will have to follow your brother foot like a good boy."

He found a hollow log to build his fire and cook his mush in his stewpan hat. "Here," he said to his feet, "we will rest." And his feet were glad.

The owls that always followed him in the evening lighted in the tall firs and the snow shook down silently. He built a fire and was cooking his mush with some nuts he had gathered, when he heard a loud coughing in the other end of the log and the unhappy face of a mother bear rose from it, looking at him angrily.

She had four little bears in the other end of the log and the smoke was making them all cough.

"Excuse me, Mrs. Bear," Johnny said, "I'll move."

So he put out his fire and moved away.

Once in the summer a mosquito flew into his fire and he put the fire out saying to the mosquito, "God forbid that I should build a fire for my comfort and that it should be the means of destroying any of His creatures."

He had a way of wearing one shoe, breaking the crust of ice . . .

Once, in a village in Indiana, a hornet crawled up his pants' leg, not knowing who he was, no doubt, and through this misunderstanding, stung him. Johnny carefully pushed the hornet down his pants' leg and told him to fly away home.

"Why didn't you kill the hornet?" he was asked and he answered, "He was defending himself with his God-given sting. I haven't the heart in me to step on a worm, kill a snake, beat a dog or a horse, or mistreat a man. Each one loves life in his own way, as much as you do, as much as I do."

The little fawns sat in a circle around him in the summer and he told them how to keep away from hunters, how to find the best nuts and the finest sweet grass.

After having further conversation with the partridges who had come to share his mush topped with summer honey, he would set off

*The little fawns sat in a circle around him in
the summer . . .*

through the woods singing:

> With my pack on my back,
> With my seed in my sack,
> A planter of apple seeds ever I'll be.
> Tra-la-la-la and a tra-la-la-lee
> Sowing the seeds everywhere.

At the "tra-la-lee" the little fawns would do a hop, skip, and jump. Johnny would have to shoo them home saying, "Go back to your mother. I am going West."

They would turn their round eyes to him and would prance on their high thin legs, and turning suddenly, show their perky white tails, as they bounded away home.

The people say they saw him everywhere.

My Grandmother said traders came through Licking Creek who said they had seen Johnny Appleseed in Missouri, Michigan, Indiana, and Kentucky.

Some would tell about seeing him walking with Indians in the Bad Lands. Others saw him paddling downstream in a hollow log chinked together with mud.

But everywhere he planted apple seeds. The first years he had to go clear back to

Pennsylvania to the cider mills to pick the seeds out of the apple mash again, with the men making fun of him.

But the fourth year my Grandmother said, she heard the crows cawing one morning shriller than usual, and she ran out and saw Johnny Appleseed coming through the clearing, still with a gunny sack for a coat, the same old stewpot on his head, and a big prairie wolf loping beside him.

The child ran out and stopped when he saw the wolf.

"Hello, child," said Johnny. "This is my friend, the wolf. He was caught in a mantrap and I set him free."

"Oh," said the child. "How do you do, Mr. Wolf? Your trees are very big now, Johnny Appleseed. I thinned them out for you and everyone here has an apple tree at his door, the way you wanted it."

The child went dancing ahead shouting, "Johnny Appleseed is here. Here comes Johnny Appleseed!"

But when the mothers saw the wolf they screamed and ran into their houses so Johnny had to tell him to wait at the edge of the forest.

It was soon spread around that Johnny Appleseed was in the village and the people began to come in ahorseback and in wagons and afoot to see the man who had given them apple trees.

My Grandmother said that in the evening they all got together and gave a party for him in the biggest house in town. They all sat around the big fire, under the drying onions and corn that hung from the rafters, and Johnny told them about the country that lay west. He told about how he traveled the old Indian trails from Fort Duquesne to Det-

roit by way of Fort Sandusky, one hundred
and sixty miles through the forests, hills and
valleys, planting hundreds of apple seeds,
going back to thin them out, repairing the
fences.

He told how he had met a bird man named
Mr. Audubon.

He told how he met a man in a coonskin
cap named Daniel Boone, along the Indian
trails.

After awhile he said, "Now do you want to
hear some news from heaven?"

He took his Bible out of his blouse and he
read to them, there, in Licking Creek, on the
edge of the wilderness.

This is what he read: "In the morning, sow
thy seed and in the evening withhold not
thine hand, for thou knowest not whether
shall prosper either this or that, or whether
they shall be good alike. God giveth the in-

The child went dancing ahead shouting, "Johnny Appleseed is here."

crease.''

They all liked the reading so much that Johnny said since there were not many books in Ohio he would share his with them. So he broke the book into three parts and gave the parts to the families and told them to pass the parts around amongst them.

He said there must be reading in America.

The people of Licking Creek, Ohio, made him a present of a leather bag for his seeds.

He would sleep in no bed but lay down beside the dying fire, after he had taken his friend the wolf a bite to eat. He said he would be off at the crack of dawn.

And the child covered him over.

My Grandmother said she got up very early in the morning and was waiting for him at the forest's edge. She said it was a sight to see him walking through the sleeping town, a pig at his heels, the chickens and geese talking to him, and a billy goat who had taken a fondness for him nibbling at his coat tails.

My Grandmother said to him, "Johnny, winter is coming on and from the coats of the animals it is going to be a hard one. You can't walk into the North without a coat."

She held up her husband's wedding coat, fine and warm, made Quaker style with bright silver buttons.

"Why," said Johnny, "I have a coat."

"Where?" my Grandmother asked. "That old sack!"

"As good clothing as any man needs," Johnny said.

"Put this coat on," my Grandmother said and almost everyone obeyed my Grandmother.

"Take these shoes," my Grandmother said.

"I have a shoe," Johnny said.

"Whoever heard of going around in the snow one shoe on and one shoe off?"

"It saves a shoe," Johnny said.

"Take these stout shoes," my Grandmother said. "I don't want to be thinking of you when the winter winds blow, walking in your bare feet through the snow."

"My feet, ma'm, are the feet of my animal friends now. Do they ever want for a shoe?"

She said it was true as day, his feet were horny like an animal's now.

"Good day to you," he said, and walked onto the ferry with the wolf. She heard him singing, the buttons of his new coat flashing in the rising sun.

When the wintry winds blow
Over the earth white with snow
Where else can you find such delight?

'Tis a joy most complete,
Mellow apples to eat,
Round the fire on a cold winter's night.

My Grandmother said she looked back and there were hundreds of little apple trees in the clearing all come from the seed he had planted that day many years before, and now there would be apple seeds at Licking Creek, Ohio, and he would not have to go back to Pennsylvania any more, where the men were laughing at him.

She said the next day an old trapper came into town and what do you suppose—he had on her husband's wedding coat and she was going to have him locked up for stealing it, but the old man swore Johnny Appleseed had given it to him saying, "Take it. Your need is greater than mine."

"That man," my Grandmother would say,

"didn't he beat all?"

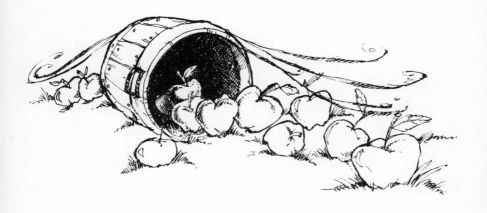

By now he knew the old Buffalo trails and the Indian trails.

He knew some Buffalo too and some Indians.

He had gone upstream on the Muskingum, planting his seeds there.

He followed White Woman Creek and then went up the Mohican into the Black Fork.

He had seen a long black river called the Missouri pouring into a longer river called the Mississippi.

One day he met an Indian whose shoulder was torn open right down to the bone.

Now the Indians all knew Johnny Appleseed, the man who carried no gun, the man who knew all the herbs in the forest, and who walked barefoot through the snake country. They knew when they were hurt he could make them well.

They also had taught him many things, too. They taught him how to make a swinging hammock high in the forest trees where he could sleep and sing all day long, swinging high above the forest floor. They had taught him new songs to sing.

When Johnny saw the Indian with his shoulder slashed to the bone he said, "I'll fix it."

They built a very hot fire and Johnny heated the long spike of his hoe in it and then put the hot metal straight into the open wound. The Indian knew this would be good and he would get well.

Johnny cooked him some mush and they told many tall stories as men do everywhere, and the Indian pointed to Johnny's long black hair and said, "Fine scalp."

They both laughed and Johnny pretended he had lost his scalp and began jumping around until the loons laughed from the river.

As you know, the Indians were very angry with the white people for coming into their land and they often fell upon their lonely cabins. Every house was far away from every other house and sometimes the Forts where the soldiers lived were far away from the settlers.

One day Johnny came into a settlement where the women were all weeping. The Indians were coming to attack the village. Someone must go through the dark that night, to the Fort and bring back the soldiers.

Johnny Appleseed knew the way all over the continent of North America in the dark. So he set out for the Fort, knocking on the doors of the cabins on the way, crying out, "The spirit of the Lord is upon me. The Indians are on the warpath. He hath anointed me to blow the trumpet in the wilderness. Flee for your lives!"

At midnight he came to the Fort and set out with the soldiers leading them back to the village and they got there just before the Indians attacked.

But Johnny would not fight his friends the Indians.

He lay under a persimmon tree and watched the battle.

Johnny cooked him some mush and they told many tall stories as men do everywhere . . .

When many were wounded he began to help them. A bullet hit him square in the middle.

"Are you killed, Johnny Appleseed?" the children cried.

He took out the big book he had in his blouse and there was the bullet gone clean through the book but it hadn't scratched his skin.

Now many apple trees stood up in the wilderness and bloomed in the spring and bore heavy red fruit in the fall and the apples were eaten in the winter in the cabins while the coyotes howled on the hills.

On such nights by the warm fires the children would ask about Johnny Appleseed. "Is he warm? Is he safe?"

And the mothers would answer, "Save all your seeds for Johnny, in the spring he will be coming back this way. He is warm. He is safe. He is one of the pure in heart."

He was warm and he was happy.

He was safe.

He had gone now into Kentucky where they had no apple trees.

Now he was in Kentucky and one day he sat waiting for his eggs to boil and he heard a quick strong stroke of an ax nearby. Someone was felling trees and he never stopped to rest at all. One tree after another fell.

Johnny thought, "There's a strong man for you." He left his cooking and went through the thicket and found a tall man in buckskin pants too tight for him, swinging an ax.

"You're a pretty good log splitter," Johnny said.

"I get practice," the tall man said, "I bought a rifle in partnership and have to split enough logs to pay my share."

"You're a tall man for your height," Johnny says. "Why you're six inches taller than I am if you're an inch."

"I'm seven inches taller than you are," says the tall man, "and I'm over an inch."

They measured heel to heel and head to head and sure enough it was so, the tall man was seven inches taller than Johnny. He wore a linsey-woolsey shirt and buckskin pants too short and skintight.

"Well, I'm as tall for me as you are tall for you," Johnny said. "Give me the other ax and I'll show you how to fell trees."

They both took an ax and the chips flew. Johnny's tree went down first.

"Say," says the tall man, "you're a regular alligator horse. We should go into partnership."

"No," Johnny said. "I'm a planter of seeds."

"Are you Johnny Appleseed?" the tall man asked.

"The same," Johnny said. "What's your handle?"

"My name's Abe," the tall man said, "Abe Lincoln."

"Well," Johnny said, "you're a rail splitter all right. Keep it up, Lincoln, and maybe you'll be President some day."

"I'm afraid my legs reach the ground too late," Abe said.

"I'll bet my eggs are burnt to a frazzle,"

They measured heel to heel and head to head . . .

Johnny said.

"You remind me of a shuttle, Johnny Appleseed, going to and fro with your seeds and your books and I'm glad I met you."

"Same here," Johnny said. "I'm glad I met you, Abe Lincoln. So long. Be good."

Johnny was barefoot and so was Lincoln.

It was many years later and the spring had come warm and early. Johnny Appleseed was older now but he still went tough and strong, walking through the wilderness, always keeping ahead of the settlers, always planting his apple seeds.

Now the animals knew him from border to border of the **Big Plains**. Above him flew his friends, the birds.

Beside him walked the four-legged friends, the deer, the bear, and even the wild hog.

And far down in the tall grass and the short grass, the tiny eyes of quails, worms, snails, all the creeping, crawling, stinging ones, watched his long lean legs going by like scissors in the morning and the evening light, apple seeds in his pouch, his stewpot on his head, his books bulging his gunny-sack blouse, and his long, horny feet gently walking the earth.

"Look out," the grasshopper would hop, "get out of the way of old Johnny Apple-seed."

The snakes would silkily drop into the water and wait until he had passed.

The ladybugs would shake their heads in alarm because in the coldest weather he would have one shoe on and one shoe off.

"That man," the ladybugs would say like my Grandmother, "he does beat all!"

My Grandmother said that the child had

tended the apple trees Johnny had first planted, and now they rose into the air for miles around and in the spring the blossoms were like an inland sea.

She said one day, in the afternoon, when the village which was now a town, was full of the fine sweet scent of apple blossoms heating in the sun, Johnny Appleseed walked down the street with a deer walking with him.

She said she saw him walk straight to the apple orchard which stood now like a bride in the sun. The child, who was now a man, came and stood beside him and they both stood there for a long time looking at the thousands of trees in bloom.

"You have done well," Johnny said to the child who was now a man. "An apple orchard is the finest thing in the world. How many trees in the orchard now?"

"Fifteen thousand."

"Fifteen thousand friends and they say I am a lonely old man!"

My Grandmother said that for all she knew he was wearing the same old sack, and he was thin now but not bent at all, his hair was gray and hung to his bony shoulders under his stewpan hat, and his toes, she said, were like tree boughs and his skin was burnt and beaten by sun and rain, but she said it was the eyes that held you.

It got about that Johnny Appleseed was in town and the farmers began to gather from miles around, and by evening the whole town was full of people who had been made glad by an apple tree. They all met in the big barn and there were such "goings on," my Grandmother said.

There was venison and ham roasting on the fire. And apples roasting in the ash. And kegs of apple cider sweet as young girls. And monstrous apple pies to make your mouth water.

And they all raised their glasses of cider, "To Johnny Appleseed!"

There was dancing, my Grandmother said, by the young plump girls, until the rafters rang. There was the hoe down, the four-handed reel, square sets and Old Dan Tucker until the poor fiddler was like to drop.

And Johnny sang to them, sitting under the strings of apples.

O, the bright golden apple,
The rich juicy apple
That hangs from the old apple tree,
Fills the heart with delight
For each apple you bite
O, the rich juicy apple for me.

And down the earth came the strong, sweet scent of the apple blossoms on the warm wind of a new world, the wind that blew then over North America, which was no longer a wilderness.

And they all raised their glasses of cider, "To Johnny Appleseed!"

Johnny had traveled a long way in a long time.

Now instead of the wilderness of silence, there were the voices of thousands of people and the ax rang out cutting down the trees making the wheat country.

The trails became highways and the sound of the stagecoach horn was heard.

The apple trees grew now and were harvested. Johnny carried them far into the sun. He always kept ahead of the settlers with the animals, wearing the morning light, far west.

He walked along the country.

The robins with their tiny eyes saw him.

The rabbits saw him between their long ears.

The deer waited for him where they had run from the hunter.

And the buffalo at evening stood in the dark of their great herds, waiting to ask him, "Where to? What now, Johnny Appleseed?"

For the towns and the cities had come now.

And the Rocky Mountains sat at the brink of the prairies.

The animals laid their heads on Johnny's knees and said, "Where are we going now, Johnny Appleseed?"

America was growing up. America was to become a mighty nation by the time you were born.

When one thing comes another thing goes.

So to make room for the people the animals had to go.

The Little Brother of the Beasts had to go.

The Indians had to go, too.

But in a hundred thousand miles north and south, east and west, the apple trees grew, raising their tide of blossoms in the spring, dropping their golden apples in the fall.

Sometimes with his back against the Rockies, waiting for the sun to come across the prairies, Johnny could smell, on the long wind of the plains, all of his trees, the fine sweet odor of their blossoming and the deep rich scent of their fruiting.

There are some who say—and my Grandmother is one of them—that they still see Johnny Appleseed at dusk, in the apple

*There are some who say they still see Johnny
Appleseed at dusk . . .*

orchards of the Middle West, singing along in his old gunny sack, his stewpot on his head, his shirt sticking out in front where he carries whatever book he is reading.

My Grandmother says that the birds fly over his head.

The owls call him from the dark.

And the little fawns leave their mothers to walk after him.

MERIDEL LE SUEUR was born in Murray, Iowa in 1900 and has spent most of her life in the Midwest. Her father was the first Socialist mayor of Minot, N.D.; her mother ran for Senator at age 70. After studying at the Academy of Dramatic Art in New York, the only job she could find was as a stunt artist in Hollywood. Her writing career began in 1928 when the populist and worker groups were re-emerging. While writing stories in the early thirties which gained her a national reputation, she reported on strikes, unemployment frays, breadlines, and the plight of farmers in the Midwest. She was on the staff of the *New Masses* and wrote for *The Daily Worker, The American Mercury, The Partisan Review, The Nation, Scribner's Magazine,* and other journals. Acclaimed as a major writer in the thirties, she was blacklisted during the McCarthy years as a radical from a family of radicals. Among her many published works are *North Star Country, Crusaders, Corn Village, Salute to Spring, Rites of Ancient Ripening, The*

Girl, and *Ripening: Selected Work, 1927-1980.* The books for children by Le Sueur include *The Mound Builders, Conquistadores, The River Road: A Story of Abraham Lincoln, Chanticleer of Wilderness Road, Sparrow Hawk, Nancy Hanks of Wilderness Road,* and *Little Brother of the Wilderness: The Story of Johnny Appleseed.* She currently lives in Saint Paul, Minnesota.

SUZY SANSOM wanted, above, all, to bring freshness and her own unique drawing style to the character of Johnny Appleseed in a way that would complement Ms. Le Sueur's charming retelling of the story. An illustration major at the Academy of Art College in San Francisco, Sansom works mostly in mixed media with an emphasis on pen and ink drawing, and has recently experimented with three-dimensional illustrations using such materials as clay, found objects, and wood. She keeps drawing journals of daily experiences which aid her in becoming more expressive in her art. This is Ms. Sansom's first storybook.

JOHNNY APPLESEED was the name given Jonathan Chapman (1775-1847), an American pioneer who planted huge numbers of apple trees along the early frontier. He was born in Leominster, Massachusetts and all that is known about his boyhood is that he had a habit of wandering away on long trips in search of birds and flowers. His first recorded appearance in the Midwest was around 1800 when he was seen drifting down the Ohio in a canoe loaded with decaying apples which he used to plant apple orchards on his rounds as a missionary. It is said that he would travel hundreds of miles to prune his trees which were scattered throughout the wilderness.

Wherever he went he read aloud to anyone who would listen from the Bible and from the works of Emanuel Swedenborg—an 18th century Swedish scientist and Christian mystic. Indians regarded Chapman as a great medicine man; he did indeed scatter the seeds of many reputed herbs of healing including catnip, hoarhound, and pennyroyal.

During the War of 1812, he once raced on foot 30 miles through the Ohio wilderness to summon American troops to Mansfield, Ohio thwarting an Indian raid.

About 1838 Chapman gradually crossed into northern Indiana and continued his missionary and horticultural services. But after a long trip to repair damages in a distant orchard he was overtaken by pneumonia and died near Fort Wayne, Indiana.

The tales and legends about Johnny Appleseed became widely known after an article describing his deeds appeared in *Harper's New Monthly Magazine* in 1871. More recent biographies of Johnny Appleseed include *Johnny Appleseed, an Ohio Hero,* by W. A. Duff and *Johnny Appleseed: Man and Myth* by Robert Price.